Two Short, Odd Plays About Faith

Granite

AND

Aardvarks and Hillbillies and an Angel Nearby

BY LOWERY CHRISTOPHER COLLINS

TWO SHORT, ODD PLAYS ABOUT FAITH

===

Granite

AND

Aardvarks and Hillbillies and an Angel Nearby

BY LOWERY CHRISTOPHER COLLINS

Ponderlake
Publishing

TWO SHORT, ODD PLAYS ABOUT FAITH:
GRANITE
AND
AARDVARKS AND HILLBILLIES AND AN ANGEL NEARBY

Written by Lowery Christopher Collins

Ponderlake Publishing: www.ponderlake.com

Playwright and/or Royalty Information: www.ChristopherCollinsOnline.com

ISBN 978-1-7349926-6-3

Granite
by Lowery Christopher Collins

Characters: LEE and TOMMY, both 23 years old

Scene: Graveyard

Tommy, a young man, out of breath, walks up.

TOMMY.   (*Looking at a tombstone*) Here it is. (*Pauses*) It's been a while.

Lee, another young man, walks up.

LEE.   Here you are.

TOMMY.   You knew where I was coming.

LEE.   Yeah, but I didn't know you'd run here.

TOMMY.   I didn't run. I just walk faster than you.

LEE.   Whatever. It's been a long time since I've been here. (*Looking around*) I can't believe
that I'm in a cemetery in the middle of the night.

TOMMY.   Ahh! Don't be such a chicken!

LEE.   I'm not a chicken. It doesn't *bother* me. It's just not a place to be after
sunset.

TOMMY: It isn't? (Pause) There's something mesmerizing about a cemetery,
especially at night. It's one of the most REAL places there is.

LEE.   Are you sure you're okay?

TOMMY.   I'm fine. In fact, this place is making me feel better.

LEE.   That makes one of us.

TOMMY.   (*Laughing*) Come on! (*Looking around*) It's not that bad.

LEE.   No, I actually enjoy sitting in a graveyard around midnight. It's a happening place. Why go out to eat? Movies should be obsolete. TV-- amateur! Look what people, well, most people, are missing! Picnic area . . . Reading material . . . Plenty of company!

TOMMY.   Either you're making jokes because you're scared to death or you have a really twisted sense of humor.

LEE.   Probably neither one. I'm not going to lie to you. This isn't my idea of a fun place to visit. It's one thing to visit during the day! An evening visit's just . . . creepy.

TOMMY.   It could be you're uncomfortable with the "plenty of company" you referred to?

LEE.   Nah. These are just empty shells. These were real people. It's amazing! Each one here breathed, slept, ate, laughed, cried, and everything else we do. And now, nothing. It's over. Just empty people. Gone.

TOMMY.   Every grave holds somebody's baby, even if they were 100 when they died. Think about it. Look at all of the graves. Hundreds of them. All of these were people like you and me.

LEE.   Yep. But each one had to face the curtain call.

TOMMY.   What a call! (*Silence*) And most of these I don't even know. I've lived here longer than I can remember, and yet, they look so unfamiliar. (*Looking*) Wait a second. There's a familiar name. She must have been related to Jerry. And see that one? That's Lisa's grandfather, isn't it?

LEE.   (*Looking*) Yeah, it is. He died last year. Remember?

TOMMY.   Yeah, but I didn't go to the funeral. I didn't know he was buried here.

LEE.   I knew they put him here, but I didn't know exactly where. I didn't go to the funeral either.

TOMMY.   I haven't been here in a while.

LEE.   Neither have I.

TOMMY.   It's just too painful. (*Walks over to the original grave that he first approached*)

LEE.   I haven't been here in a least three years.

TOMMY.   (*Staring at the grave*) It's been longer than that for me.

LEE.   I guess I figured that it didn't accomplish anything to visit.

TOMMY.   I wonder what Adam would think if he knew we were standing over his grave?

LEE.   I don't know. If he were alive, he'd probably make a joke of it.

TOMMY.   (*Laughing*) Yeah, like, "Hey, off-a my toes, guys!!"

LEE.   (*Smiling*) Or he'd tell us we were blocking the moon, ruining his tan!

TOMMY.   You know, I wonder what he would have thought five years ago if he knew he'd be here today?

LEE.   That was the last place on his mind then.

TOMMY.   I guess it's the first place now.

LEE.   Five years today.

TOMMY.   Yeah. It's strange to see today's date on a tombstone.

LEE.   It's even stranger to see Adam's name there. It's like seeing your own.

TOMMY.   Five years. (*Pause*) Boy, what five years have done! It isn't fair. Lee, it isn't. Look at that chunk of granite. You know, life is like that rock. Hard, etched letters, a weight upon your head. Pretty to look at, but a constant reminder of death. A . . . sign of sorrow and unhappiness. A granite rock announcing the end. Look at that, Lee. That's what's left of Adam. A gray rock.

LEE.   A gray rock. (*Silence*) Five years. And to think that when we die, that's all that's left for us. Granite. Adam was a great guy. Funny. Smart, well, not dumb. Everybody who knew him loved him, and just about everybody knew him. There's *still* not a week goes by that I don't hear his name mentioned. Granite. If he knew that granite marked his life he'd probably throw a fit. With everything he was and everything he did, this piece of gray granite stands for him?

TOMMY.   Well, Lee, what *should* stand here? A truck? A stereo? A basketball? Those kinds of things were his life. You can't stick those in the ground to be monuments for him.

LEE.   I know, but those were the things that would be more fitting. This rock, monument, this looks like every other gravestone out here, makes him seem just like everyone else out here. He wasn't like them.

TOMMY.   He wasn't?

LEE.   No, you know good and well he wasn't. I know that this place is filled with good people, people who were important to their families and friends, fathers and grandfathers, mothers and grandmothers, but Adam, (*Pause*) well, it's just different. Adam was special. Adam was our friend. It couldn't have been his time, yet.

TOMMY.   No, it doesn't seem fair. It could have been any of us. (*Pause*) You know, maybe a truck, a radio, or a basketball would have been a more fitting monument to him.

LEE.   Those were his life. (*Pause*) Well, let's be honest here. If either of us had been put here five years ago, those things would have fit us, too. It's amazing how five years can change people.

TOMMY.   You're right.

LEE.   I don't spend time on the same things today that I did five years ago. I don't even think the same way.

TOMMY.   Same here, but to me, Adam will always be that same guy.

LEE.   That's what death does, freezes us in time. We'll always remember Adam at eighteen. Even when we're eighty, he'll always be eighteen.

TOMMY.   You think he would have changed by now?

LEE.   It's hard to imagine, but yeah, probably, some, I think so.

TOMMY.   All this is hurting my brain. (*Pause*) It seems like last week that he came over to the house and we all went hiking in those woods behind the barn.

LEE.   You talking about that time we found that coral snake?

TOMMY.   (*Laughing*) Yep, I thought he was going to climb that tree right by the creek!

LEE.   But then Michael *fell* in the creek!!!

TOMMY.   (*Laughing*) Was that really almost seven years ago?

LEE.   Let's see . . . Yeah, if not more. (*Thinking*) Yeah, seven years.

TOMMY.   You know, for years I've listened to my grandparents talk about the "good old days." I always listened respectfully, but I've always thought about how long ago it was and how it didn't really matter anymore. But, as young as I am, I catch myself looking back the same way. Seven years seem like a snap of the fingers.

LEE.   Yeah, and I remember when it seemed like forever between my birthdays. I thought I'd be a kid forever. Now, things are flying by. (*Silence, looking at the tombstone*) How can it be five years ago today?

TOMMY.   That's what the granite says.

LEE.   Can granite lie?

TOMMY.   No, I don't guess.

LEE.   Where do you think he is?

TOMMY.   What do you mean?

LEE.   I mean, where do you think he is?

TOMMY.   About six feet under there. (*Points at the grave*)

LEE.   No, I mean where do you think Adam is, not his body, his . . . soul!

TOMMY.   I thought we weren't going to discuss things like this!

LEE.   That was five years ago. We've grown up. You said it yourself. Where do you think he is?

TOMMY.   Lee, he's in the ground. I don't wanna talk about that mumbo jumbo. He's dead.

LEE.   So, everything that was Adam is dead? Granite is all that's left?

TOMMY.   Adam lives on in us, Lee!! In our memories.

LEE.   You've *never* thought about where he *is*? Come on, I know that his death was one of the most traumatic experiences that ever happened to either of us. Even the people he made fun of cried and thought they'd lost a dear friend, but time marches on. Can you tell me you never wondered where he is?

TOMMY	Heaven, Lee. Heaven, okay? Adam was a good guy. A little wild, a little crazy, a lot of fun. If he is anywhere, he's gotta be in Heaven. God had probably been waiting for him to liven the place up. Harps, clouds? It needed a few jokes.
LEE	Why are you trying to make this a joke?
TOMMY.	Who's trying to make what a joke? Adam lives in Heaven. In one of those mansions of gold. He probably has a basketball embedded with diamonds, drives a Rolls Royce with Heaven's best stereo system, bouncing along the streets of Paradise. Adam's Heaven! All his dreams come true. *(Laughs, pauses)* Why aren't you laughing?
LEE.	It's not funny. I'm worried. I don't know where Adam is.
TOMMY.	What do you mean? You're not suggesting he went to the other place, are you?
LEE.	I don't know what I'm suggesting. All I know is that Adam did some pretty wild things. He wasn't "bad," by any means, but he wasn't what you'd call a Christian.
TOMMY.	Of course not! He wasn't one of *those* people. Mamby pamby people who live on cloud nine. Weak. Just weird. People who can't cut it in the real world. He was a real guy, a good guy, a good friend, a fun friend, and you know it. He was Adam. He was a regular guy.
LEE.	Where do "regular guys" go when they die?
TOMMY.	Well, to "regular guy" Heaven. Where normal people go. Like I said, Adam was a good guy. He never hurt anybody. Well, not much anyway. And not people who didn't deserve it, not people who didn't need to learn to lighten up and live.
LEE.	How do you get into "regular guy" Heaven? Any entrance fees? Regulations?
TOMMY.	What's into you? Where is all this coming from?
LEE.	I'm just thinking, Tommy. He's laid here five years with a block of granite over his head. Twenty years from today, we could still be visiting here and it'll be the same. He died at eighteen and has the same marker. I'm just thinking there's something more to it. Where is he, really?
TOMMY.	Lee, he's gotta be in Heaven!

LEE.	Remember his grandmother at the funeral. She kept crying and saying that her baby never accepted "Jesus."
TOMMY.	Oh, Lee! You know grandmas. They're overemotional. That's part of the job description. They focus on all that stuff. They're old. Their lives are over.
LEE.	I can't get her words out of my head.
TOMMY.	Hey, hey! Remember the preacher talking about Adam walking through . . . Paradise in the Beautiful Garden?
LEE.	He was talking about "THE ADAM," Eve's husband in the Garden of Eden, not our Adam!
TOMMY.	Oh. I thought he was talking about our Adam. Did he ever say where he went?
LEE.	No, he couldn't have. He doesn't know. Even if he thought Adam didn't go to Heaven, what is he going say? "Dear friends, I'm sorry to inform you that your loved one is in hell today." "Hey everybody, he's just burning away." Huh? No.
TOMMY.	That would be a bit harsh.
LEE.	To say the least.
TOMMY.	I'm really confused now. *(Pauses)* He can't be in . . . hell. I know he made fun of religious people, but that was just funny. He was joking . . . he was just being Adam. I'm so confused.
LEE.	*(Pointing at the grave)* I know this is going to sound selfish, but I don't want to end up like him!!!
TOMMY.	Well, I have news! We all die.
LEE.	You've missed the point again. I know I'll die, but I want more of a legacy, not just "oh, he was a fun guy! Oh, he sure did make us laugh! Oh, he was a good friend!" What kind of legacy is that? It's just like that block of granite! And for all we know, he could be in hell.
TOMMY.	Why do you keep saying that? That's not funny. He was our friend!
LEE.	Exactly! And what do you think our friend would tell us now if he could? Would he have done anything differently? What did his popularity get

	him? His possessions? His "fun times"? Would he warn us not to end up where he is?
TOMMY.	Have you taken some preacher's correspondence course or something?
LEE.	No, everything had just gotten a lot clearer here. I'm glad we came out here.
TOMMY.	Clearer? It's anything but clear. I really don't understand any of this. Adam was my friend. I miss him. It's really hard to accept that he's been gone for so long. And I really haven't wanted to think where he went when he died. It hasn't really crossed my mind much.
LEE.	And why do you suppose that is?
TOMMY.	What?
LEE.	Why do you think it hasn't crossed your mind much?
TOMMY.	I don't know. It just hasn't.
LEE.	Could it be that if you thought about where Adam went, you might have to wonder where you'd go if the same happened to you?

Silence.

LEE.	It's so much easier to ignore the truth than to deal with it. And we don't want to deal with it if it means we have to make decisions about our lives.
TOMMY.	Did you like swallow a Bible before we came out here tonight?
LEE.	No, but I think years of Sunday School and other things have come to mind over the last few minutes.
TOMMY.	I don't remember much about Sunday School except the hypocrites there.
LEE.	Tommy, we're not talking about them! Look!!! (*Points at the grave*) You can't blame any hypocrites for that. There are no hypocrites around. He's dead. They have nothing to do with it. Granite. Right? That's it! It could have been different. But we can't change the past. We can chance the direction we're headed though. If one of those trees fell on us right now, we would you be?
TOMMY.	Well, there and there and there and there . . .
LEE.	Tommy! You know that if a tree that big fell on us, we wouldn't be in

several pieces! We be nailed in the ground like a couple of fence posts. But the point is, we'd be dead!

TOMMY.   True.

LEE.   But, then where would you be?

TOMMY.   In that plot over there? *(Points across the graveyard)*

LEE.   You know what I mean.

TOMMY.   Yeah.

LEE.   Where, Tommy?

TOMMY.   I don't know, Lee. Before tonight, I assumed we'd join Adam for a game of dominoes, but right now, I don't know.

LEE.   It's time to grow up, Tommy. I have a feeling that I know where I'd go, and I don't like it. As for me, I think I need to do something about it. A monument of granite isn't good enough. I want more of me to live on than that. Deep down inside I know that God does love us. I think it's time for me to love Him back. I owe Him. I do think it's time. I'm going to see that preacher that lives by the church. I need to talk to Him.

TOMMY.   It's almost midnight! It's late.

LEE.   Exactly. It's late. I don't wait until too late. *(Starts to walk away)*

TOMMY.   Wait!! I'm coming, too. Whew, this makes me nervous!

LEE.   You don't have to come.

TOMMY.   I want to, really.

LEE.   Okay. We have some business to tend to. *(Smiling)* I can't take life for granted anymore.

TOMMY.   *(Rubs the tombstone)* Yep. Sorry, Adam. I wish you could come with us, but . . . you know.

LEE.   It's getting late, Tommy. We have a preacher to wake up.

TOMMY.   Let's see if he wears pajamas with little crosses on them?

They begin walking offstage.

LEE: Are you serious?

TOMMY: Me? Always.

LEE.   I figure he'll have entire little churches on them, steeples and all.

TOMMY.   That'd be pretty cool.

They exit.

Aardvarks and Hillbillies and an Angel Nearby

A Peculiar Christmas Tale

written by Lowery Christopher Collins

Cast of Characters

Barry Boyett   --a reporter with *The Washington News*

Emma Boyett   -his wife

"Maw" Arboreen   --matriarch of a Southern family

Simmy Jo Arboreen --her nine-year-old daughter

Harlan Arboreen   --Maw's nineteen-year-old son

Sheriff Fred Bolling--"the law in these parts"

The Angel   --a Heavenly guide from God

Act 1

Friday evening, December 24, 1943. Approximately 6.00 p.m.

Scene 1: In the wilderness

BARRY.   C'mon! C'mon!

EMMA.   I'm coming!

BARRY.   C'mon! You're too slow. What are you doing? Taking your time?

EMMA.   Don't you take that tone with me, Barry Boyett!

BARRY.   You're as slow as Christmas!

EMMA.   Christmas is here, Barry! Christmas is here!

BARRY.   I don't care. You're slow.

EMMA.   It would be best if you were just quiet now. These heels are killing me. We're in the middle of who knows where. There are probably wild animals everywhere around us.

BARRY.   Lions, tigers, bears, snakes, aardvarks . . .

EMMA.   Aardvarks? Did you say aardvarks?

BARRY.   There could be aardvarks out here.

EMMA.   Aardvarks?

BARRY.   Aardvarks.

EMMA.   You're crazy. Aardvarks don't live here. Not (*raising her hands*) here!

BARRY.   Why not? Why couldn't they live in . . . in . . .

EMMA.   Where? Where are we?

BARRY.   Well, the car broke down right at the border. We're either in Georgia or Tennessee.

EMMA.   Georgia or Tennessee?

BARRY.   Or Alabama.

EMMA.   You don't even know what state we're in?

BARRY.   Georgia. We're in Georgia. We haven't walked that far yet. No, we drove across that small river. Georgia!

EMMA.   Are you sure? It feels like we've walked through ten states!

BARRY.   You're slow and difficult.

EMMA.   I'm going to hit you. Yep. I'm going to hit you. Do you realize that we left Maryland five days ago? Five days! You said that five days would be more than enough time to drive to Houston. Sure, plenty time! Well, Barry! It's December 24th! Christmas Eve! Christmas Eve 1943! And we're stuck in the middle of Backwoods U.S.A.! The middle of nowhere! Aardvarks!!!

BARRY.   Are you through?

EMMA.   Maybe.

BARRY.   Maybe not.

EMMA.   I think you're going to be through. Where are we?

Scene 2: The Arboreen Porch

SIMMY JO.   *(singing)*
            Jimmy Crack Corn and I don't care.
            Jimmy Crack Corn and I don't care.
            Jimmy Crack Corn and I don't care.
            Tomorrow is Christmas Day!

MAW.   *(sticking her head out of the door).* Hush, child! Your brother is trying to sleep!

SJ.   Sorry. *(Maw goes back inside. Simmy Jo walks around a little bit and starts singing loud again.)*
           Jimmy Crack Corn and I don't care.
           Jimmy Crack Corn and I don't care.

MAW.   Simmy Jo, your brother's just back from fighting that Hitler feller, and he's tryin' to sleep!

SJ.   Sorry! *(Maw goes back inside. Simmy Jo looks at the sky.)*
           Christmas. Christmas! Christmas Eve!!!
           (Emma and Barry walk up.)
           Maw! Maw!!! There's strangers here!!!!!
           (Simmy Jo runs into the house.)

EMMA.   Where are we? Where are we?

BARRY.   Calm down, Emma. There's a house. I'm sure there's some nice people here.

EMMA.   Aardvarks?

Maw comes onto the porch.

MAW.   Howdy.

BARRY.   Hello, ma'am. My name's Barry Boyett. This . . .

MAW.   Arboreen.

BARRY.   Ma'am?

MAW.   This is the Arboreen Place. Twenty generations strong. People call me "Maw."

BARRY.   Well, Mrs. Arboreen, Maw, we're lost. Our car broke down several miles back yesterday about noon, and we've been walking since daylight today. Until now, we haven't seen a sign of life anywhere.

MAW.   Well, you sit down and rest a spell then. Sit down, girly. It's okay.

EMMA.   Thank you.

They all sit.

MAW.   Y'all two married?

EMMA.   Yes, ma'am. We've been married a little more than a year.

MAW.   A year? A year?!? How old are you, anyway?

EMMA.   Twenty-three.

MAW.   Twenty-three years old?

EMMA.   Yes, ma'am.

MAW.   Lord, have mercy! When I wuz yor age, I'd been married over eleven year! You didn't get married 'til you wuz twenty-two?!? Heavens to Betsy Ann Jenkins, you must be lucky! Most old maids don't get a chance after fifteen.

EMMA.   Fifteen?

MAW.   Twenty-two? Whew, girly.

EMMA.   Where I come from, girls wait and finish school and then start thinking about marriage later.

MAW.   I nearly finished, girly. My sister graduated the schoolhouse at twelve and then got hitched.

MAW.   Schoolhouse?

MAW.   Schoolhouse.

BARRY.   You'll have t' overlook my missus, ma'am. She tain't been 'round much.

EMMA.   Barry, stop that!

MAW.   Don't think nothing of it. She's just green fer her age. Marriage'll fix that.

EMMA.   This is some nightmare. Barry, I'm going to make you pay. Your future is dim.

MAW.   It's still daylight, girly.

BARRY.   Yeah, your sight's going, Emma.

MAW.   Emmer? Your name Emmer?

EMMA.   No, it's Emma.

MAW.	Well, I'll just paint a pig green and call it Sadie! My sister's name is Emmer. That's the one I wuz tellin' ya 'bout. The one which finished her schoolin'.
EMMA.	How pleasant.
MAW.	No! She hain't pleasant! She's a cantankerous one! Done kilt three husbands.
EMMA.	Barry! Barry! I want to go home!
MAW.	Don't you worry none, deary. She hain't 'round here. She's done moved to Huntsville.
BARRY.	Huntsville?
MAW.	Huntsville, Alabama. Way out west. I hain't never been that fer, though.
EMMA.	Alabama? Did you say Alabama? Is that the state we're in?
MAW.	I don't rightly know.
EMMA.	You don't know?
MAW.	Reckon not.
EMMA.	You don't know what state you live in?
MAW.	Naw. Those fancy men in the blue suits came out with some fandangled sticks and string. I don't reckon we ever found out if we's in Alabama, Georgia, or Tannersee. We still hain't heerd.
EMMA.	Barry, if we ever get to Houston, I can promise that you'll never finish paying for this.
MAW.	Did you say "Houston"?
EMMA.	Did you hear me, Barry?
MAW.	Did you say "Houston"? Houston, Texas?
EMMA.	Oh! You've heard of it? Texas. A big state nobody never gets to.
MAW.	Jumpin' Jimmy Jefferson! Y'all been to Houston?

BARRY.   That's my home.

MAW.   Really! Your home? That's a fer piece, hain't it?

EMMA.   Evidently, it's "ferther" than I thought!

MAW.   You hain't never been there?

EMMA.   No. Probably never will.

MAW.   Houston wuz where my boy, Harlan, hadta go to catch one-a them big-wing "air-o-planes" to go cross't the water to fight.

BARRY.   Your son's a veteran?

MAW.   No, sir! We's all Democrats here. Nothin' but!

BARRY.   I mean he fought in the war?

MAW.   Yes, sir. 'Til he got shot. One-a them Hitler fellers got him in the arm. Then he wuz hurt in a wreck on the way to the hospital. But he fought like a true Arboreen!

BARRY.   You should be very proud. I'm a correspondant for *The Washington News*. I'm constantly at the front, and I can tell you . . .

MAW.   Why hain't you over there now?

BARRY.   I'm currently on a short leave. I came to see my wife and family.

MAW.   *(to Emma)* You don't go with yer husband?

EMMA.   No, ma'am. I don't go to the front with Barry.

MAW.   A strange sort. Both of you.

EMMA.   Barry, I want to go home. I'm tired. I'm hungry. I smell.

MAW.   If you's hungry, we got some viddles in the kitchen.

EMMA.   No thank you. I'm not that hungry.

Simmy Jo comes onto the porch.

SJ.   Maw! Harlan's woke up. I think he's wanting some vittles.

MAW.   Well, pull out the 'coon leg, Simmy Jo! Pull out the 'coon leg!

EMMA.   I think I'm going to get sick.

MAW.   Simmy Jo, bring out the fish oil. This woman's getting sick! You going have a kid?

EMMA.   No. I'm not. And I'm fine! Barry, I'm asleep. I have to be. Why don't I pinch *you* and see if you scream and I wake up?

SJ.   Hey, Maw! What's wrong with that feller? He hain't got no hair!!

BARRY.   *(feeling his hair)* What?

SJ.   No! On yer face! Where's yer whiskers?

BARRY.   Oh. I ain't got none ---- I mean I don't have any.

SJ.   What kinda feller is you?

MAW.   Simmy Jo Arboreen!!! Watch yor manners.

BARRY.   *(feeling his face)* I shave. Well, normally I shave.

SJ.   What's that? Shave?

MAW.   Quit yer nosin', girl. Get the 'coon out!

Simmy Jo goes back inside.

EMMA.   *(pulling Barry aside)* Look. It's Christmas Eve. We're supposed to be in Houston tonight. These people can't help us. They need help themselves. They don't even know what state they live in. Let's just go. We're safer with the aardvarks.

MAW.   It's getting late. Why don't y'all stay with us tonight? You can sleep in the
back
            yard or in the barn.

BARRY.   We'd better go. We appreciate your offer, though.

EMMA.   You're being sensible!

MAW.   Y'all be careful, then.

BARRY.   Thank you.

EMMA.   Hallelujah!

As Barry and Emma start to walk away, the angel puts his right hand up a few feet in front of them.

BARRY.   (*Stopping*) You know, it's getting late. It might be better if we stay the night.

EMMA.   Are you getting crazier by the minute? It's just dusk!

BARRY.   No. I've just got a feeling that we should stay the night.

The angel puts up his left hand as well.

BARRY.   It's going to get dark soon.

EMMA.   (*staring to change her mind*) Eh . . . Eh . . . (*looking out into the distance*) Maybe you're right. Why are you right?

BARRY.   Mrs. Arboreen?

MAW.   Hey.

BARRY.   Can we still take you up on your offer?

MAW.   What?

BARRY.   We'd like to stay tonight if it's still okay.

MAW.   That's finer than a possum baked in pine straw! Y'all come on up. We's gonna have a Christmas shin dig!

EMMA.   So, you've heard of Christmas?

MAW.   Heerd of it? Apples baked in hog lard, girly! We got Christmas out here. Just 'cause they got lights and purdies up in them big cities like Atlanta and Flyin' Squirrel Holler don't mean we hain't got nothing 'cheer'!

MAW.   I'm sorry. I didn't see no . . . any lights or wreaths.

MAW.   We can't afford no fancy stuff like the Hatterman, the Browns, or the Johnstons, but we got all we need! We don't need no fancy store-bought tree purdies. Thanks to Mr. Roosevelt, we got 'lectricity. We hain't gonna waste it on no red or green lights.

31

EMMA.   Well, I'm sure you do well with what you have.

BARRY.   I'll bet you make a great manger scene!

MAW.   A what?

BARRY.   A manger scene.

MAW.   I'm sorry. You gonna have to cut out that city talk. I'm just country. I don't know no big fancy words.

BARRY.   A manger scene. A crib for the baby Jesus.

MAW.   For the baby?

EMMA.   For the baby Jesus!

MAW.   Aw! Are you folks talkin' 'bout that church stuff?

BARRY.   Well, yeah. The Christmas Story. Jesus. The manger. Mary. Bethlehem?

MAW.   Y'all are in to all that stuff? Eh?

EMMA.   Well, yeah. That "stuff" is real.

MAW.   It's been a good thirty years since I seen a church. There wuz one here when I first met Clyde. I wuz somewheres around Simmy Jo's age--'bout nine or ten. Anyway, I hain't thoughta one in years.

BARRY.   You don't have churches around here?

MAW.   No, sirrie! Not in this small neck of the woods. Like I wuz sayin'. when I wuz 'bout nine or ten, this preacher came into the woods and set up a tent fer a church. Then he tried to build one-a those log churches. He started sayin' all kinds of crazy things. He said we couldn't drink no squeezins or shine or even the July Brew! But he made Paw real mad when he said that we couldn't shoot our neighbors. That was just plum foolish! Can't shoot yer neighbors!?! Paw'd done kilt least fifteen or twenty Jacksons and Burtons. Well, Paw and his brothers got rid of that preacher. Real quick. He wuz gone. Real! My left ear! That preacher stuff is phony! Can't shoot yer neighbor!?! We shown him! What's in the bag?

EMMA.   *(Dazed)* Huh?

MAW.   The bag, girly!

EMMA.   Just some personal things. An extra sweater. A Bi . . . Bi . . . Bye-bye
          good-night book.

MAW.   A what?

EMMA.   Nothing.

MAW.   Well, we's gonna eat and have us a Christmas time. My boy William cut a
          tree that we put some pine cones and berries on. We give the kids their
          toy fer the year, and then we eat our 'coon, possum, and sweet tators. I
          don't know 'bout none of this baby stuff, but we's doin' dandy! That's a
          word my boy brought back from Europe!

BARRY.   We celebrate the birth of Christ at Christmas.

EMMA.   Barry, maybe you'd better not . . .

The angel puts out his right hand toward her.

BARRY.   God's Son came to earth and was born in a manger. He came so that we
          could have eternal life.

MAW.   *(Confused by his words)* Eternal life?

BARRY.   Go to Heaven and live forever.

MAW.   Well, I don't know nothin' 'bout that stuff. I never even been to Scottsboro
          or Gadsden, much less Chattanooga. I've heerd of Birmingham and
          Tupelo.

BARRY.   Heaven is where Christians go after they die.

MAW.   Die? Well, after we die, us Arboreens go up to the family plot by
          Harbengerdale Crick.

BARRY.   Your body dies, but your soul lives on.

MAW.   I don't know none of that stuff. *(Changing the subject)* We have a high
          ole time at Christmas. Is your family expectin' you tonight?

BARRY.   Well, they were. They're probably worried now.

MAW.   What 'bout your family, Sister?

EMMA.   What?

MAW.   You ain't spendin' Christmas with your family.

EMMA.   No, I'm not. *(Dazed)* I'm here in . . . the woods.

MAW.   Well, you're spendin' Christmas with us now, Sister. I hope your family don't miss you none too much.

EMMA.   They know I'm supposed to be with Barry's family. But I'm sure they're eating now. Probably roast beef.

MAW.   Ooo-Eeeeeeh! You must be one-a them rich folk! One of them million-dollar folk.

EMMA.   Oh, no. My father's a . . . *(stops abruptly)*

MAW.   A what?

EMMA.   A pr . . . A min . . .

MAW.   A what? Grizzly got yer tongue? A what?

EMMA.   A . . .

BARRY.   A preacher.

MAW.   A preacher!?!

EMMA.   Thank you, Barry.

BARRY.   You're welcome.

MAW.   A preacher!?! That's what that crazy feller wuz we runned off. That's too much! How old is your paw? He wuz twenty or twenty-five then! Is your paw in his fifties? Did he send you here?

EMMA.   Whoa! No, no, no! I can promise you he don't . . I mean he doesn't know I'm here. He doesn't know where I am. He thinks I'm in Houston.

MAW.   Well, I'd hate to have to run you off, being you two is so nice. Just as long as you don't tell us how to act! *(In a brainstorm)* What do you think 'bout shootin' your neighbors?

EMMA.   Uh . . . I . . . I guess if they shoot at you???

MAW.   Answer me, boy!

BARRY.   I . . . If they deserve it, I guess it . . .?

MAW.   Okay. Just checkin'. Y'all is welcome fer Christmas as long as you keep
            those foolish church hankerings to yourself. I'm goin' inside. Y'all sit
            down and get comfortable. The rest of the men folk'll be home soon.

She goes inside the house.

EMMA.   Why did you go and tell her about Daddy?

BARRY.   I really don't know. It sort of slipped out. I'll tell you. I've been all across
            Europe and most of Asia, and I've never experienced anything like this. I
            wanted to travel to see different kinds of people, but I guess I should have
            come . . . here.

EMMA.   Wait a minute!

BARRY.   What?

EMMA.   What you said.

BARRY.   What?

EMMA.   When Daddy was in his early twenties, before he married Mom, he went
            on a mission trip all across the South setting up churches for the poor.
            That must have been 1913 or 1914. Surely, he wasn't . . .

BARRY.   You've got to be kidding! Surely, he wasn't the one she . . . There are
            churches all throughout the South. *(Thinking)* Well, I guess not
            everywhere.

EMMA.   Surely not here. Not the one they ran off. Though I'm sure it could have
            been.

BARRY.   Wow! What a story!

EMMA.   *(Half to herself)* Is there no road untraveled?

BARRY.   Wow!

Harlan, with his arm in a sling, comes onto the porch.

HARLAN.   Hey, I'm Harlan.

35

BARRY.   Hey.

EMMA.   Hello, Harlan.

HARLAN.   I guess you folks is the city folk gonna et Christmas with us'n?

BARRY.   We's guessin' so.

EMMA.   *(Giving Barry a hard look)* Yes, if you don't mind.

HARLAN.   Aw, naw. That's fine. Maw tole me you wuz out here. She said you just got back from Europe.

BARRY.   Yes, I'm a reporter for *The Washington News.*

HARLAN.   I just got back two weeks ago myself. I wuz hurt. Got my arm shot and then crushed. On the way to the doctors. In a bus crash.

BARRY.   I'm sorry. How long were you over there?

HARLAN.   Well, I left in March. I got back two weeks ago. They said I couldn't fight no more. I shot a lot of folk though.

EMMA.   I don't doubt that.

BARRY.   Well, I heard your family's planning a big Christmas.

HARLAN.   Yep.

BARRY.   Food and presents and music?

HARLAN.   Food and presents, but no music. Us Arboreens ain't too musical. Never been.

EMMA.   Well, I have some Christmas music in my bag I was taking to Houston. Maybe we could sing some.

HARLAN.   Maybe you could. We ain't singers. Anyway, none of my family can read the words to 'em.

BARRY.   Can you read, Harlan?

HARLAN.   A little. I went to the grade school some and learned the letters and sounds. And there was this real nice guy in the service who taught me to read a little more. He taught me to read signs and a little from some books.

EMMA.   That's great. I love reading. You read any books recently?

HARLAN.   We ain't got none here. I'm the only one that can read. And I ain't real
             good at it. Your paw's a preacher?

EMMA.   *(Surprised)* Well . . . yes. News sure travels fast.

HARLAN.   Hmmmm. My family's always been 'gainst that stuff. But that feller that
             taught me to read them books in the service, his paw wuz a preacher, too.
             We read some outta that book, that black Bible book. Pretty interesting
             stories in there.

EMMA.   It's pretty interesting reading. I've got one . . . *(hesitates)*

The angel raises his right hand.

EMMA.   I have one in my bag. *(She takes out her Bible.)*

HARLAN.   Really? Can I see it?

EMMA.   Sure. Here.

HARLAN.   *(He opens the Bible and with great difficult slowly reads from Luke
             Chapter 2)* "And it came to pass in those days, that there went out a
             decree . . ."

BARRY.   Oh, the Christmas Story!

HARLAN.   The Christmas Story? In here? I ain't read this part.

EMMA.   It's the second chapter of Luke. The Christmas Story. Christmas night.
             Appropriate.

BARRY.   Coincidental.

HARLAN.   In the Bible? Christmas has to do with God?

EMMA.   Christmas is all about God! The birth of the Christ Child. Read, Harlan,
             read!

HARLAN.   Here. *(He hands the Bible back to her.)* If Maw seen me reading anything
             to do with church, she'd skin me alive and toss me in the pond.

EMMA.   But . . .

MAW'S VOICE.   Harlan, you out there with them city folk?

Emma quickly puts the Bible back in her bag.

HARLAN.   Yes'm, I'm out here.

MAW'S VOICE.   Tell 'em 'bout Europe.

HARLAN.   Done did.

MAW'S VOICE.   Harlan?

HARLAN.   Yes'm?

MAW'S VOICE.   Your paw and yer brothers just came in the back door. You and them city folk, come in. Let's eat!

HARLAN.   Come on in. It's viddle time. The 'coon's a-calling. Come on. Come on. Let's eat. When I wuz in Europe, I missed Maw's 'coons. Yer in fer a treat.

Barry and Emma slowly go inside.

EMMA.   I'll bet. Barry, I'll bet a lot of things.

End of Act 1

Act 2

Scene: The Arboreens' front porch

Barry and Emma come out on the porch.

BARRY. You can tell our grandchildren that you ate baked "'coon."

EMMA. Barry, if I were you, I'd be quiet.

BARRY. And pine-straw-baked possum legs!

EMMA. Hush!

BARRY. It's amazing what hunger will do to a person. And sweet potatoes seasoned with
pig feet and squirrel tongue!

EMMA. Barry!

BARRY. We still have a dilemma. We're in the middle of nowhere.

EMMA. And it's Christmas Eve.

BARRY. And it's Christmas Eve.

EMMA. I still can't get over the fact that Daddy might possible have been the preacher
they ran off years ago.

BARRY. Well, as far as the food goes, he's better off for not having stayed.

EMMA. We've got to do something to let these people know what Christmas really is, who God is! Maybe if we were to talk to them, to witness to them?

The angel shakes his head.

BARRY. I don't know if that would work. Mrs. Arboreen probably wouldn't allow it. She seems pretty hard about that, especially toward strangers.

EMMA.   Well, I feel burdened, but I feel so helpless, though! *(She walks around.)* It's Christmas, Barry!

BARRY.   Yep. *(He stares at the ground.)*

EMMA.   *(Singing)* "Silent Night, Holy Night, All is Calm, All is Bright."

HARLAN.   *(Entering)* Hey, you're singin'!

EMMA.   *(Startled)* Yeah, a Christmas carol.

MAW.   *(Entering)* Hey.

HARLAN.   Hey, Maw. Emmer's singin'!

MAW.   Singin'? Emmer, you singin'?

EMMA.   Well, sort of.

MAW.   Go on. We don't hear much singin' 'round these parts.

BARRY.   Go on, Emmer!

EMMA.   *(Hestitant)* "Silent Night, Holy Night." *(She pauses.)* "Deck the halls with boughs of holly! Fa la la la la la la la la!"

MAW.   I'll be a deep-fried guinea sewed up in a tow sack! I hain't never heerd nothin' like that afore!

EMMA.   It's a Christmas song.

BARRY.   A secular one.

MAW.   What's that mean?

EMMA.   Nothing. Just a kind of song.

BARRY.   Yes, it is.

EMMA.   *(Singing once more)* "Silent Night, Holy Night." (*clearly distraught*) Barry, I can't. Not now. It's not right yet.

MAW.   You city folks is crazy! You know that?

EMMA.   Barry, I know we need to send the light, go forward with the Great

Commission, but not this way. Not now. It doesn't feel right here, now. Not yet. You're right. It would backfire, now.

MAW.   Whew! You city folk is somethin' else!

Simmy Jo comes out onto the porch laughing. She's holding a stick that has been crudely fashioned into a doll of some sort.

SJ.   I ain't never got me a doll afore! My own stick doll! See my doll, Emmer!?!

EMMA.   Whew! I mean "wow!" It's a stick doll all right. It's pretty, honey. (*Relaxing*) It's pretty. I hope you enjoy it.

BARRY.   Harlan, have you had a good Christmas?

HARLAN.   Yeah, I guess.

BARRY.   Something wrong?

HARLAN.   Naw, I'm just thinking 'bout Christmas. That holiday thing. (*whispering to Barry*) That Christmas Story? The first Christmas?

BARRY.   Yep. It's a great story!

MAW.   What y'all talkin' 'bout?

HARLAN.   Aw, nothin'. Christmas, presents, dolls.

Emma is rocking the stick doll as if it were a real child.

MAW.   You got a present!

HARLAN.   I know. I've always wanted twelve nails.

MAW.   I hunted high and low fer them things!

HARLAN.   I know, Maw. Thank you.

SJ.   (*to Emma*) Wuz you singin'?

EMMA.   Yes.

SJ.   I sing!

EMMA.   You do?

41

SJ.   Uh huh!

EMMA.   Would you like to sing for me?

SJ.   Maw?

MAW.   Go 'head, child.

SJ.   *(singing)*
            Jimmy Crack Corn and I don't care.
            Jimmy Crack Corn and I don't care.
            Jimmy Crack Corn and I don't care.
            Tomorrow is Christmas Day.
            (Melancholy)
            Tomorrow is Christmas Day.

BARRY.   *(Softly)* That's great.

EMMA.   *(Echoing)* Tomorrow is Christmas Day. Tomorrow *is* Christmas Day! It's
            Christmas, people! The Christmas season! The most special time of the
            year!

HARLAN.   Look! It's Fred Bolling!

MAW.   I'll be if it hain't Sheriff Bolling!

EMMA.   *(in shock) Sheriff* Bolling!!!

BARRY.   *(also in shock)* In a car!?! A 1932 Ford!?!

EMMA.   In a car? This is the sheriff? Someone who knows where he is?

BOLLING.   Hey, folks! Just ridin' 'round. Makin' sure everybody's o.k. Y'all all
            right?

MAW.   We're great, Fred. We got company, too.

BOLLING.   Really? Howdy, I'm Fred Bolling. Moonshine County Sheriff.

BARRY.   Sheriff, my name's Barry Boyett. We're . . .

BOLLING.   The reporter from Washington?

BARRY.   *(Elated)* Yes!

BOLLING. You and yer wife has been on the radio. Your folks called in and they've had bulletins all over the South. They said you wuz missin'. You shoulda been in Houston. Had trouble?

BARRY. Yes, sir. We have. Is there any way we could ride with you back to a town?

BOLLING. Yes, sir. We'll fix y'all right up.

Simmy Jo begins taking all the belongings out of Emma's bag.

EMMA. Glory be! Oh, sir?

BOLLING. Ma'am?

EMMA. What state are we in?

BOLLING. *(a little confused)* Alabama, ma'am.

EMMA. Okay. Thank you. *(to Maw)* Alabama. You live in the state of Alabama.

MAW. Okay. Alabama.

BARRY. We'll get our things.

BOLLING. All right.

EMMA. Mrs. Arboreen, thank you for a . . . for a meal.

MAW. You're more than welcome, girly. And . . . Simmy Jo, what in Eleanor's name are you doin'? You ought to be ashamed!

Emma's bag is completely empty.

EMMA. That's okay.

MAW. Naw, it hain't. She's a-meddlin'! *(Maw gets up.)*

EMMA. Don't worry. It's Christmas. There's nothing personal here.

HARLAN. There's one or two good things, though. Some music. A . . . a book.

EMMA. It'll only take a second to pick all this up.

The Bible is the last item on the porch. She starts to pick it up, but the angel puts his finger on it, holding it down. She tries again but is met with the same resistance. She thinks. She looks at Harlan. She looks at Barry. Barry nods. She picks up the Bible and hands it to Harlan.

EMMA.   Here, Harlan. Keep this. I don't care. Keep it. Read it.

BARRY.   The book of Luke. Chapter Two.

MAW.   What's that?

HARLAN.   *(Hesitant, but then with new-found courage)* A book, Maw. A book I'm gonna read. A book I started a while back. I'm gonna finish it now.

BARRY.   Good reading, Harlan.

HARLAN.   Much obliged!

EMMA.   Read every day.

HARLAN.   I will.

EMMA.   Merry Christmas, y'all. We're going to Houston. And Barry's not driving.

MAW.   Good night, Sister.

SJ.   Bye.

BARRY.   Bye.

Barry and Emma leave with the sheriff.

MAW.   *(Curiously looking over at Harlan)* Now, what's that book, Harlan?

HARLAN.   A great book, Maw. Sit down. I know you don't wanna hear this, but I want you to listen. I'm readin' to you 'bout the first Christmas night. I'm readin' it out loud. I'm readin' it now. *(With great difficulty, he reads from Luke 2)* "And it came to pass in those days, that there went out a decree from Caesar Augustus that all the world should be taxed . . ."

Lights dim.

End of Act 2 and End of the Play

Lowery Christopher Collins (Chris) has been an educator and writer for over thirty years. He is currently a professor of English at Panola College in Carthage, Texas. He has taught at the high school, middle school, and elementary school levels and as an English and literature instructor at the college and university level. For several years, he was a high school theatre director and a gifted education consultant. He's been honored with several teaching awards, including the Young Audiences of Northeast Texas Outstanding Service to the Profession Award and the Kennedy Center's Steven Sondheim Award for being one of the most "Inspirational Teachers" in the U.S.

He is also an award-winning playwright of over thirty scripts, a weekly newspaper columnist, a short story writer, a poet, a pianist, a vocalist, a songwriter, a recording artist with Daywind Studios, the founder and artistic director of Stagelands Theatre Company, an aspiring novelist, and a (former) choir director. He's taught a variety of classes, from rhetoric and composition to literature to acting to the Bible.

He holds a Bachelor of Arts Degree in English and History and a Master of Arts Degree in English from Stephen F. Austin State University in Texas and has served on fine arts and gifted education committees as well as on a board of governors for a small playhouse.

In addition to his interests in teaching, directing, and writing, he has a fondness for lighthouses, windmills, filmmaking, salsa, sculpture, Flannery O'Connor, travel, dominos, guacamole, social media, genetics, Maine, landscaping, pillows, gospel music, Shakespeare, marbles, YouTube, quantum physics, movies, weird jokes, maps, trees, cold rooms, and Texas.

He can be reached at mrchriscollins@hotmail.com,

on Facebook at www.facebook.com/tofferdreams,

on Twitter at "tofferdreams,"

and at his website: www.ChristopherCollinsOnline.com.

To view Christopher Collins's books and other writing, visit Ponderlake Publishing, at www.ponderlake.com.